Refugee children tell their stories in words and paintings

One day we had to run!

Sybella Wilkes

Evans Brothers Ltd Evans in association with **UNHCR** and **Save the Children**

Contents

The terms 'refugee' and 'displaced person' are both used in this book. These definitions may help you:

What is a refugee?
A refugee is someone who has fled across a national border from his or her home country, or is unable to return to it, because of a well-founded fear that he or she will be persecuted for reasons of race, religion, nationality or political opinion. Refugees who cross borders because of famine are not necessarily covered by international protection, unlike a refugee fleeing from war etc.

What is a displaced person?
A displaced person is someone who has been forced to move to another part of his or her own country because of war, famine or disaster.

◄ **Opposite:** painting by Liban Ahmed Habib, aged 10 years, Ethiopian, Ifo refugee camp. "The Somali old men are all waiting outside the school saying, 'Paint this, say this, don't say this, don't paint this.' I think it is very funny."

Evans Brothers Limited
2A Portman Mansions
Chiltern Street
London W1M 1LE

© in the maps Evans Brothers Limited 1994
© in the text, photographs and children's paintings Sybella Wilkes 1994

Printed and bound in Barcelona, Spain by Cronion, S.A.

ISBN 0 237 51489 3

Project editor: Su Swallow
Editor: Nicola Barber
Design, maps & page make-up: TJ Graphics
Production: Jenny Mulvanny

The photographs and paintings in this book are the property of the UNHCR. All the photographs are reproduced with the permission of **Panos Moumtzis** with the exception of the following: **Fiona McDougall** p9, 47 & 58 (top right); **J. Mohr** p37 (right); **Betty Press** p17, 25 (middle left), 30 & 50; **Wendy Stone** endpapers. p16 & 51 (left). The author wishes to thank: Sironka Averdung, Care International, Jacaranda Designs, Louisa Lockwood, Nina Joachim Trust (Durham University, UK), Radda Barnen, Alabel Derib, John Mungai, Stephen, Refugee Council, Jill Rutter, Save the Children Fund, UNHCR, Ian Lethbridge, Panos Moumtzis, Millicent Mutuli, Lois Williams and, of course, **all the refugee children who told their stories and painted their pictures for this book**.

The Author, Publishers and organisations associated with this book wish to point out that whilst every effort has been made to ensure the accuracy of the information presented here, that information does not necessarily reflect the views of the Author, Publishers or said organisations.

Foreword

This book communicates in a direct and vivid way the experience of a group of young refugees in the Horn of Africa. It not only records the tragedies witnessed by the young contributors, but is also a celebration of their lives and cultures. Looking through their eyes we can experience some of the dramas they have survived, the bewilderment they feel at being refugees; but also their optimism for a better future. We have much to learn from their words and pictures and their courage in communicating their experiences to us is greatly to be admired.

Whilst these are personal stories, the experiences they relate are not unique to refugees in one corner of one continent. All over the world increasing numbers of children are to be found in refugee camps as a result of war, famine and drought.

Helping the world's 20 million refugees is the job of the United Nations High Commissioner for Refugees (UNHCR). Considering the fact that more than half the refugees are vulnerable, defenceless children, this is a daunting task. Very importantly, UNHCR protects refugees from physical harm and from being forcibly returned to their country. Food, shelter, water and medical care are the next life-saving priorities that UNHCR rushes to provide to refugees in every situation. Beyond these basic needs, UNHCR encourages education and training programmes for refugees.

Upholding the rights of children everywhere to special care and protection is a central plank of all Save the Children's work. It was Save the Children's founder, Eglantyne Jebb, who wrote the world's first charter on children's rights which many years later, in 1989, was to inspire the UN Convention on the Rights of the Child. Save the Children organisations around the world have been at the forefront of moves to improve the standards of care for refugee children.

This book is an important contribution towards a greater understanding of what it means to be a child refugee in today's world. I commend it to anyone who, for whatever reason, has an interest in the welfare of children and recognises the importance of preparing them to play a responsible role as adults in society.

Anna Ford

Children's words; children's brushstrokes

The stories and pictures in this book are written and painted by refugee children in Kenya. They were done so that children in other parts of the world could understand what it is like to be a refugee. The stories are the children's own words; the pictures the children's own brushstrokes.

It is very difficult for these children to deal with the emotional horrors they have experienced. The idea that 'a problem shared is a problem halved' does not really apply to children. Many find it hard to put how they feel into words, and are reluctant to discuss their experiences. I found the Sudanese children particularly difficult to talk to. Robbed of their childhood innocence by the civil war, they were scared to talk in case they said anything that their elders disapproved of. They often repeated well-rehearsed phrases about the 'condition of Sudan' which told me nothing about their own feelings and experiences. Many of the children found my questions stupid and obvious: yes, of course they

had seen dead and dying people, so what? But when asked, "How do you feel about this?" they would withdraw into themselves and refuse to reply.

However, it was the children who helped me to find a way of communicating. Having spent several awkward hours with a group of Somali children who were telling me how they had reached Kenya, one of them said to me, "Why are you asking so many questions?" When I replied that I wanted to tell their stories to other children in the world, they brightened up enormously.

"Do you think they would like to hear the story about the lion that was larger than a camel and faster than a horse?" asked one of them.

Children who had previously been bored and shy came to life. I realised that if we

had fun together I would learn more about them and they would learn to relax. Wherever I went after that I carried an armful of comics and story books. I would tell them the stories that I had heard as a child and, in return, they would tell me their own stories and fairytales.

I worked with a Kenyan artist, Sironka Averdung, to teach the children how to use paints. Painting gave these children a great freedom of expression. They would queue up with their pictures, wanting to tell me 'their story'. One boy was very keen that "the children of the world know that my picture is about the suffering of Sudan". The children found it less disturbing to relive their memories through their artwork than in words.

Sybella Wilkes

Where do refugee children come from?

Why do these countries suffer from famine?

Famine in the Horn of Africa (see map p11) has brought much attention to this region. Pictures of suffering have appeared on television screens and in newspapers all over the world. Many people now connect the countries of Somalia, Sudan and Ethiopia with war and famine. But why do war and famine go together in these countries?

Many people live a 'hand to mouth' existence in the Horn of Africa. They depend entirely upon the crops they grow and the animals they keep for food. When their lives are disrupted by war they are often forced to abandon their precious crops and animals. Famine and disease can easily become greater threats to the population of a country at war than the fighting itself. Many of the children of Somalia, Sudan and Ethiopia die, not directly as a result of the war itself, but from a lack of food.

Refugee children are children without a country or a home. Sometimes they no longer even have a family. They are children without a childhood.

As these children flee conflict, hatred and persecution, they see terrible suffering. Sometimes they are abandoned in the panic to escape, or are forced to take sides in wars they do not understand. Already shattered by the loss of their homes, possessions, and often their entire way of life, the long journey to safety can be even more traumatic for refugee children. They may face danger, exhaustion and misery every step of the way. Many refugee children know what it is like to be hungry, day after day.

Refugees: a worldwide crisis

Over the last 40 years, the numbers of refugees have increased dramatically. When the United Nations High Commissioner for Refugees (UNHCR) was set up in 1951 there were one million refugees in the world. Today, there are about 20 million refugees. This reflects the growing instability in the world today. It is frightening to think that during the last four decades, 20 times more people have been forced to flee their homes as a result of war, persecution and famine.

Every day, somewhere in the world, children become refugees. Of the 20 million refugees in the world, over half are children. They flee their countries because their lives are in danger. This book records the dreams, the nightmares, the stories and the fairytales of refugee children. It also tries to explain some of the reasons why these children are refugees.

Refugees in Africa

There are about six million refugees in Africa, the largest number of refugees in one continent in the world. This book concentrates on the lives of refugee children in the Horn of Africa – the north-eastern region of Africa that juts out between the Red Sea and the Indian Ocean. During the past 30 years the Horn of Africa has experienced a constant refugee crisis. In 1992, more than 400,000 people flooded into Kenya to escape civil wars in Somalia and Sudan, and instability in southern Ethiopia. The stories of the escape of three children, from Somalia, Sudan and Ethiopia, form the basis of this book. The civil war in Somalia is being fought between rival clans battling for power and territory. As a result of this civil war, ten per cent of the Somali population lives outside the country's borders.

Meanwhile, the fighting in the civil war in southern Sudan became so fierce that, in May 1992, 20,000 Sudanese people fled to Kenya. About half of these refugees were young boys, most separated from their families. They had run away from home to escape the bombardment of their villages. These children are a living example of the way that children become the main victims of every war.

Finally, a happier story. In November 1992, 40,000 Ethiopian refugees in camps at Walda and Banissa in Kenya began to return home. An agreement between the various clans of the Oromo in Ethiopia meant that, at last, the refugees felt safe to go back to their own country.

Chronology

1956 Sudan gains independence. By 1958, civil war is raging between the north and south and southern Sudanese flee to neighbouring countries.

1972 Agreement made between the government of Sudan and the tribes in the south. Hundreds of thousands of southern Sudanese refugees return to Sudan.

1978 Somalis living in Ethiopia flee to neighbouring regions as the war between Somalia and Ethiopia rages over the Ogaden region of Ethiopia. Over 500,000 people are forced to flee.

1983 People leave southern Sudan as the civil war between the north and the south begins again. By 1990 an estimated 400,000 refugees have escaped to Ethiopia, as well as Uganda, Zaïre and (in 1992) Kenya.

1985 Tens of thousands of Ethiopians go to Sudan to flee civil war and famine.

1988 Tens of thousands of Somalis flee as war breaks out in northwest Somalia. The Ethiopians who had been refugees in this area either return home, or go to Kenya. By December 1990 there are 375,000 Somalis in Ethiopia.

1991 Refugees from southern Sudan are forced to leave Ethiopia after the fall of the Ethiopian leader, President Mengistu.
Fighting is widespread across Somalia. By 1992 one million people have fled to Kenya, Ethiopia, Djibouti and Yemen.

1992 Ethiopian refugees in Kenya begin to return home.

1993 Some Somali refugees feel safe to return home in time to plant crops on their land.

Sudan The past

The name Sudan is short for Bilad as-Sudan which means 'land of the black people'. Originally, this was the name given to all black African countries south of the Sahara. It was only in the 19th century that the name Sudan came into use for the country we know today.

In ancient times, gold was mined in Sudan. The pharaohs (kings) of Egypt built settlements there to protect Upper Egypt, and to exploit the gold mines. Egypt's influence lasted many centuries, and during the 19th century Egypt established a network of provincial governments to keep control over Sudan. Sudanese attempts to become independent began early in the 1880s when an Islamic leader, the Mahdi (meaning 'Messiah'), began a war to claim Sudan from the Egyptians and their British rulers. The Mahdi managed to drive out both the Egyptians and the British, but these two powers later joined forces to regain Sudan. Their victory in 1898 resulted in joint British and Egyptian rule until independence in 1956.

Sudan is the largest country in Africa, and the ninth largest in the world. It is often considered to be divided into two parts – a northern Muslim half and a southern half where people follow Christian or traditional African religions. When Sudan was a colony the two halves were ruled as separate territories, and since independence in 1956 there have been many problems between the people of northern and southern Sudan. The Arab (Muslim) north dominates the African (non-Muslim) south because it is richer and more developed. After independence,

civil war raged in the south, claiming an estimated 500,000 lives and forcing hundreds of thousands more people to leave their homes. The government of Sudan spent much of its money on weapons to fight the war, rather than on its starving and homeless people.

In 1969, Colonel Nimeri took over government and managed to end the civil war by promising the people of the south some independence from the north. An agreement made in 1972 paved the way for many refugees to return to southern Sudan. However, in 1983, Nimeri overturned this agreement and imposed strict Muslim laws upon the entire country. This led to the resumption of the civil war.

In the south, the Sudanese People's Liberation Army (SPLA) was formed, and it has been at war with the government of Khartoum (the capital of Sudan) since 1983. Since 1992, the SPLA itself has split into two groups which have been at war with one another. Hundreds of thousands of people have fled from Sudan

Sudan The present

into neighbouring Ethiopia, Uganda and Kenya. People have also left their homes and travelled to other parts of Sudan. These refugees are known as displaced people, and they are often in an even worse plight than those who have left the country. Villages may be trapped by fighting, making the delivery of food supplies very difficult. Some areas are too dangerous for relief workers to enter, and often the only way to get food to displaced people is by dropping it from planes. No one knows how many displaced people are in Sudan – some estimates put it at nearly three million. Many are suffering from hunger and disease. Most are living on the brink of disaster, always ready to flee the next attack.

The situation in southern Sudan is still getting worse. The estimated three million displaced people trapped in Sudan could flood across the border to Uganda, Ethiopia, Zaïre or Kenya at any time. But there are already 42,000 Sudanese refugees in Ethiopia, 28,000 in Kenya, 150,000 in Uganda and 135,000 in Zaïre.

In 1988, relief workers in southern Sudan observed thousands of boys walking towards Ethiopia. They were coming from the western Upper Nile and Bahr el Gazal, hundreds of kilometres away. Already separated from their families by their jobs as cattle herders, these boys trekked east along the Nile and Sobat rivers until they reached Ethiopia. Most were fleeing attack from government troops. But as well as seeking peace and security, they were also leaving in order to go to school, as many of the schools in southern Sudan had been closed because of the war. Education is an important goal for these boys. Relief workers often reported seeing exhausted and starving boys clutching their only possessions – books.

In the refugee camp at Panyido in Ethiopia, the Sudanese refugee boys lived in dormitories and were given the education and security that they longed for.

However, when the Mengistu government fell on 27 May 1991 (see page 47), they were forced to flee back to Sudan. They found their home country as insecure and devastated as when they left it. For three days the boys were on the run. Many had to cross the Gillo River; the water was high and fast-running after the rains and, overhead, planes were dropping bombs. There was much horror and confusion and many of the children were washed away and drowned.

Many of the boys settled for a while in Pochala and Nasir in southern Sudan. But there was always the threat of further attack, and they were soon moved to Narus. Here, food was scarce and even basic survival was difficult. In another attempt to provide safety for the boys, they were again moved to Kenya. After three months in a camp at Lokichokio, they arrived at their present home at Kakuma refugee camp in northwest Kenya.

Chol Paul Guet and his travels

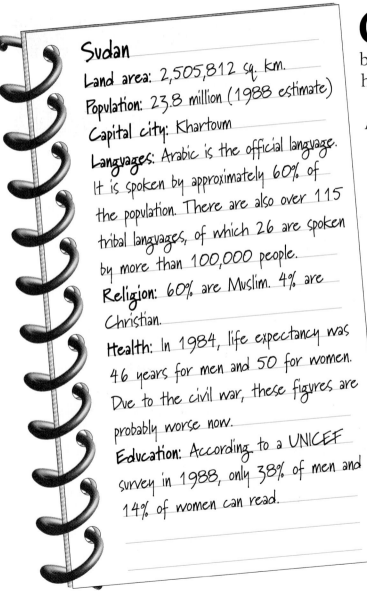

Sudan

Land area: 2,505,812 sq. km.

Population: 23.8 million (1988 estimate)

Capital city: Khartoum

Languages: Arabic is the official language. It is spoken by approximately 60% of the population. There are also over 115 tribal languages, of which 26 are spoken by more than 100,000 people.

Religion: 60% are Muslim. 4% are Christian.

Health: In 1984, life expectancy was 46 years for men and 50 for women. Due to the civil war, these figures are probably worse now.

Education: According to a UNICEF survey in 1988, only 38% of men and 14% of women can read.

Chol comes from Sudan. He is a confident and independent boy, and unlike many of his friends he speaks good English and Swahili.

After I met him, Chol ran away from Kakuma to the capital of Kenya, Nairobi, for two weeks. He said he wanted to find a better education for himself. He returned because, "Nairobi is a very dangerous place."

Chol was happy to talk about his walk from Sudan. It took a while to find out the 'true' story, however, with some versions including heroic tales of fighting lions! Chol is one of many Sudanese children desperate to have a good education.

Chol Paul Guet, aged 14, Sudanese, Dinka Bor tribe.

Chol's journey

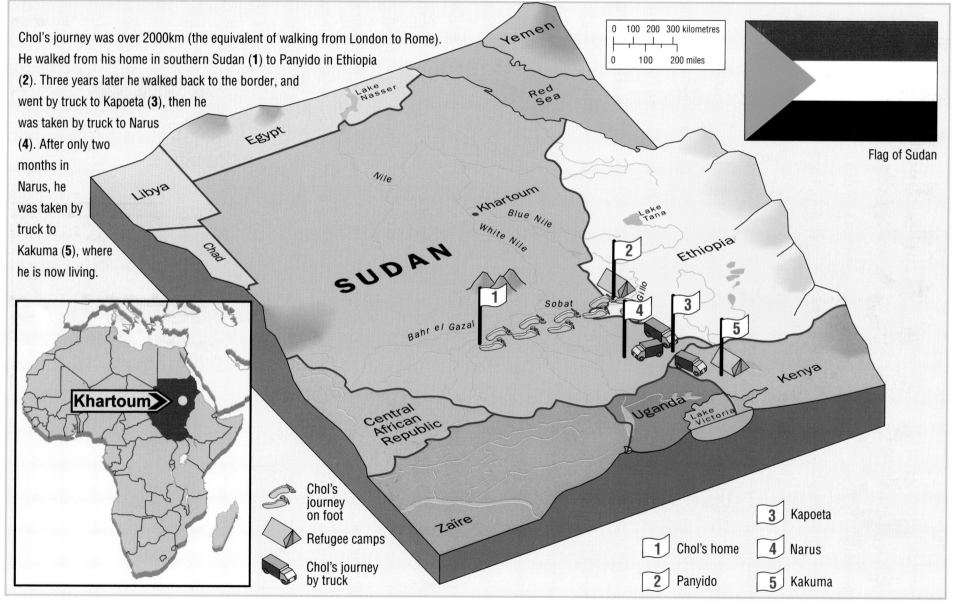

Chol's journey was over 2000km (the equivalent of walking from London to Rome). He walked from his home in southern Sudan (**1**) to Panyido in Ethiopia (**2**). Three years later he walked back to the border, and went by truck to Kapoeta (**3**), then he was taken by truck to Narus (**4**). After only two months in Narus, he was taken by truck to Kakuma (**5**), where he is now living.

Flag of Sudan

0 100 200 300 kilometres

0 100 200 miles

Chol's journey on foot

Refugee camps

Chol's journey by truck

1	Chol's home	**3**	Kapoeta
2	Panyido	**4**	Narus
		5	Kakuma

Something like an accident

"It was something like an accident when I ran away from my village. We were playing at about 5 o'clock when these people, the soldiers, came. We just ran. We didn't know where we were going to, we just ran. The soldiers divided into two groups; one for the village, one for our herds of cattle. My brother helped me to run. We didn't know where our mother or father were, we didn't say goodbye. When there is shooting, when you hear BANG! BANG! BANG!, you don't think about your friend or your mother, you just run to save your life.

I didn't see the soldiers, I just heard the shooting, the screaming and the bombing that went DUM, DUM, DUM, DUM like this and killed many people. It all just happened, like an accident, and we ran without anything – nothing – no food, no clothes, nothing.

In the day the sun is hot and your feet burn. So we walked at night when it is cold, because then you don't say all the time, 'I want water, I want water.' To rest we stood under trees, but you can die of hunger if you give up and just lie under a tree.

Wild animals, lions, killed many people. You see, when you stay behind and say, 'I don't want to do this walking, this running, I just want to sit,' the lion will kill you. But I was not scared because I was with many people, and when the lion came we would shout, 'Huh! Huh! Go! Go!' and then the lion would not kill us.

"I was not scared because I was with many people."

So we just walked. We ate soil and the leaves of trees. The big boys knew the way. I think God showed us the way. You see, when you have God he says, 'Go this way' to the good people. But without God you could go this way, that way – and where do you go?

On the roads you can't leave a person who just sits down. You must pinch him and say, 'Get up! Get up!' God has told you that you must take this person, he is life. How did I keep walking? When I saw a small boy walking I would say, 'See this small boy? He is walking.' And I would carry on. We would tell stories to make us happy, saying, 'We are going to get food, we will be happy.'

We never felt well. We just walked.

> **On the roads you can't leave a person who just sits down. You must pinch him and say 'Get up! Get up!'**

People died of hunger. I saw many dying. Even my friend died. There was no water, no food. When I saw my friend dying I carried on walking. You see sometimes you can help, and then sometimes you can't. You are talking about your life. I had to leave my friend because I would die with him. When he refuses, when he won't go, what can you do?

After two months, we came to the Anyak tribe who knew the way to Ethiopia. They helped us get fish and make dry fish. Not bad! We would catch the fish standing in the

Desperate to learn

Something like an accident

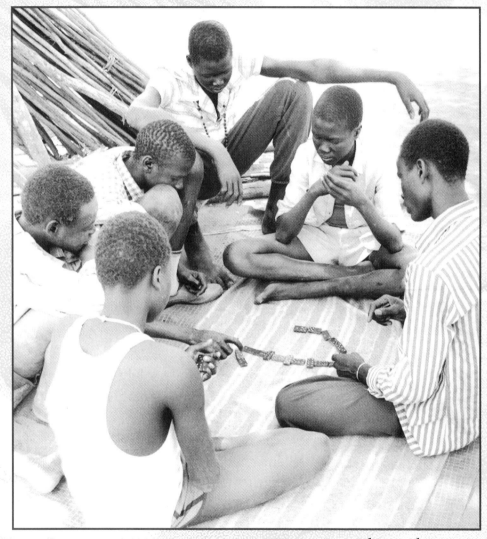

Like children all over the world, refugee children enjoy playing dominoes.

river, but ten fish can't feed five million people, and everybody wanted some. So, we would catch and give to the next person. We stood in a line in the river. Sometimes, someone would take a fish and then run away with it. But what can you do?

To go to Ethiopia, to the Panyido refugee camp, there was a big river we had to swim across. Many people drowned on the way. Some people who did not know how to swim refused to go, saying, 'We could be going anywhere, to Europe, anywhere!' When you have two or three brothers they can help. We try this way, that way, every way. There were strings and ropes to help pull people across. Many people stayed to teach themselves to swim. You see, you die if you can't swim. If the water goes over your head like this – whoosh – then you turn over and crash and die.

They gave us food, one hand like this, only one handful to last one week.

In Panyido, we did not have food for two months, but at least there was peace. Some people tried to steal the sorghum from the village, but they had to be killed. Then the United Nations, he came, he saw the people, he went to Geneva to find food, and he came back. I spent three years in Ethiopia and felt well. I went to school and lived with five other boys. Then the United Nations left and we had to run. You see, the new president of Ethiopia did not want refugees. So he came and chased the refugees away. We couldn't do anything, what could we do? It was not our country.

So, we had to swim and then swim again. Some trucks took us from the border to Kapoeta town. It took two weeks. Sometimes we would have to wait for two days at a river. They gave us food, one hand like this, only one handful to last one week. And water, dirty water and we were sick, very sick with the diarrhoea and the bump, bump of the road. At Kapoeta, after three days

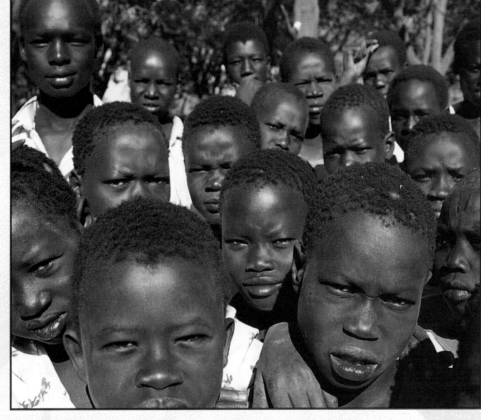
The children of Kakuma camp, fascinated by the camera and the photographer

the United Nations said, 'Take them off to Narus.' What was happening we didn't know, when we asked people they said there was fighting and bombing and the soldiers might get us. In Narus we

started building our schools and getting books, but we had to leave after only two months because of more fighting. You see, the United Nations High Commissioner for Refugees (UNHCR), he was in Kenya not Sudan, so we went to Kenya where we would be safe.

Now I live with other boys in Kakuma. We cook for ourselves and build our own homes. I like playing basketball, but there is also football and school if you would like.

We are town people now, we have shoes and a shirt, you see? I say, let us stay here where it is safe. In England you are safe, now let us stay here safely. Now we want to learn. One day I will be an engineer to build Sudan like the other countries in Africa.

I don't know whether my mother and father are dead or alive. I was nine when I left Sudan. I am 14 now. I am an oldie man now. My mother will not know me. 99

The walking of the many

Painting by David Kumcieng, aged 15, Sudanese, Kakuma refugee camp.

"We wanted to run, but we had to walk because we were tired and so hot and hungry. In my picture the people are wearing clothes, but of course we didn't have any clothes. We saw people dying, it was always the young ones, the hungry ones and the old ones."

Crossing the River Gillo

Painting by Mac Anyat, aged 17, Sudanese, Kakuma refugee camp.

"It was terrible. People shouting, screaming: 'Run, swim, go, go!' Where was my friend? He was taken by the river. Nobody was anybody's friend. How can you be a friend when people are shooting at you and the river is going whoosh — and you have to go in that river? The bang, bang and the whoosh, whoosh made my mind go dead and I don't remember who was there, who died, what happened."

Tit for tat

The camel and the fox were friends and thieves. A true friendship. One day, they wanted to cross the river so that they could go to the farm and steal food. The camel said to the fox, "Get on my back so that we can cross the river." And the fox crossed the river on the camel's back.

On the other side, they arrived at the farm. The fox caught the chickens and the camel ate the vegetables. The fox finished eating the chickens quickly because he had only a small stomach. When he had finished, he said to the camel, "After I have eaten my lunch I am accustomed to singing."

The camel, who had not finished eating because he had a large stomach, cried, "Don't sing! The farmer will hear you. Let me finish my lunch first." But the fox didn't listen, and started to sing. The men at the farm heard the singing and came running. The fox ran away quickly, but the camel could only run slowly. The men caught the camel and beat him until his bones started to hurt. When they let him go he went to the river. The

fox was waiting there because he couldn't swim.

The fox said, "Can I get on your back to cross the river?"

The camel replied, "Get up!" and the fox jumped on to the camel's back. When the camel came to the middle of the river, where the water is very deep, he said, "After I have eaten my lunch, I am accustomed to taking a bath."

The fox begged, "No, no, please don't take a bath! I will drown!"

"I'm sorry," replied the camel, "but I always take a bath after lunch." And slowly he let his backbone go down into the water.

"Help!" shouted the fox.

The camel said, "Do you feel sorry for what you did?"

"Yes! Help!" replied the fox.

The camel felt sorry for the fox. He said, "I cannot let you die," and he took the fox to the other side of the river. When they reached the riverbank, the fox and the camel both promised that they would never hurt one another again. "But," said the camel, "that was tit for tat." And they both laughed.

by Daniel Arou Diing Arou
aged 14, Sudanese, Dinka Bor tribe

Painting by Yel Awar Langar, aged 14, Sudanese, Kakuma refugee camp. "I hope that other children enjoy our stories. Sometimes I think that people think we don't laugh, we don't play. Of course we do!"

Kakuma refugee camp - the 'children's camp'

In Kakuma refugee camp, there are 25,000 children in a camp of 40,000 people. Some of these children have not seen or heard from their parents for seven years. Almost all the children are boys between seven and 15 years old, the girls having stayed behind in their villages in southern Sudan. The sad fact is that many of these boys have allegedly already served as child soldiers.

Kakuma is a very positive camp in which the boys' welfare and education is well provided for. Social workers have started a foster care project amongst the Sudanese refugees in the camp to give the boys some security. Another project to help the boys trace their parents in Sudan has also begun.

But refugee camps are not islands of peace. The political problems between the rival tribes that are fighting in Sudan are just as strong in the camp. The children feel tied to the war. For these boys, nightmares about their past experiences are made worse by their feelings of responsibility, and, sadly, many return to Sudan to fight as soon as they are old enough.

Some refugee workers are given bicycles for use around the camp. At the end of the day, their bicycles are in great demand.

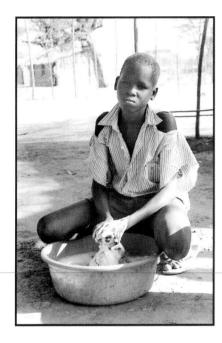

◀ Washing - a job everyone hates!

▼ Every day the boys take turns to queue up for water. Another job everybody hates!

▶ The boys cook in groups of six. They are given wheat flour, cabbage, oil and sugar.

▼ Making bricks out of mud to build a house or a school.

◀ Having fun! Many refugees are quite used to seeing journalists and photographers in the camp and are not scared to show off.

▶ Grinding wheat to make chapatis, a kind of flat bread

The party

Once upon a time, the animals decided that they would live in one group and the birds would live in another group. So, one day, the animals decided to have a party. The Zebra was the watchman. All the animals came to the party to have a happy time. Then the Bat arrived and said,

"Let me into the party, for I am an animal."

But the Zebra said, "No! We are animals because we don't have wings; you are a bird because you have wings."

So the bat left without going to the party.

The next day, the birds decided to have a party. The Vulture was the watchman of the bird party. The Bat heard the party from a long way away and decided he would go. When he arrived at the party he said,

"Let me into the party, for I am a bird."

But the Vulture said, "No! We are birds because we don't have teeth; you are an animal because you have teeth."

So the Bat had to leave without going to the party. The poor Bat was not an animal and not a bird, so he could never go to a party.

I say: tell the children of the world, we don't want to be bats. We want to find our place, to be either an animal or a bird so that we can be happy.

by Abraham Marial Kiol
aged 14, Sudanese, Dinka Bor tribe.

Painting by Zekaria Aken Deng, aged 15, Sudanese, Kakuma refugee camp.

Dinka man fighting buffalo

Painting by Simon Mac Anyuat, aged 17, Sudanese, Kakuma refugee camp.

"My picture shows a man from my tribe, the Dinka, wearing traditional clothes and fighting a buffalo to prove that he is a man."

My village in Sudan

Painting by Bor Alier, aged 17, Sudanese, Kakuma refugee camp.

"In my village in Sudan, people would come and take photographs of us and ask about our terrible life. We would tell them how we had lost our cattle, how we needed help. Then they would go away. Again and again. We thought they would help. Then one day we had to run. We had nothing. Nobody came back to help. Don't ask me about my problems. You will just go away too."

Somalia The past

During the Middle Ages, Arab merchants established trading posts in Somalia. These became Muslim centres and, as a result, most Somalis are Muslims. Most countries in Africa are made up of people from different tribes, speaking different languages. But Somalia is an exception. All Somalis share a common language, culture, and a belief that their Muslim leaders are descendants of Aquil Abu Talib, cousin of the prophet Mohammed. However, despite these common origins, the Somali people are still divided by clan rivalry. Somalia is divided into six clans, each containing many smaller groups or sub-clans. The main clans are: Dir, Darod, Issaq, Haweia, Digil and Rahanwayn.

Somalia was divided into European colonies at the end of the 19th century. One part went to the British to form the northern region of Kenya. Another went to France – this is now Djibouti. The Ogaden region was given to Ethiopia. The only parts left as 'Somalia' after the division were Italian Somaliland, with its capital in Mogadishu, and British Somaliland, with its capital in Hargeisa.

In 1960, Italian Somaliland and British Somaliland became independent and united to form one nation. Since that time there has been a move to unify all the regions inhabited by Somali people to form a 'Greater Somalia'. The five territories containing Somali people are represented by the five points of the white star on the Somali flag.

The first government that was formed after independence had representatives from all the

Muslim children learn about the Muslim holy book, the Koran

clans. However, it soon became disrupted by clan problems and in 1969 democratic rule came to an end when General Mohammed Siad Barre seized power.

In 1977, Somalia went to war with Ethiopia to try to regain the Ogaden region, but the Soviet Union (as it was then) helped Ethiopia to defeat Somalia. Hundreds of thousands of Somali people living in Ethiopia were forced to flee across the border to Somalia. An agreement between Somalia and Ethiopia in 1988 paved the way for these refugees to return home.

From the mid-1980s, rebel groups began to challenge the authority of President

Somalia The present

Siad Barre's government. The President responded by imprisoning, torturing and executing his opponents. In 1988, people in northwest Somalia were forced to flee as civil war broke out between rebel and government troops. By 1990 the fighting had spread to the capital, Mogadishu, and in 1991 Siad Barre fell from power. One of the rebel groups declared their leader president. The other rebel groups immediately rejected this.

From November 1991, the fighting in Somalia has been taking place between the various Somali groups in a struggle for power. Thousands of people have been killed in this savage civil war. Late in November 1992, the Secretary of the United Nations (UN) made the decision that it was necessary to send UN troops to restore peace in Somalia. The first American troops arrived on 9 December 1992. Unfortunately, the UN troops have also become targets for the rebel Somali groups. But by mid-1993 the situation in some parts of Somalia had improved enough for some people to be able to return home.

As a result of the civil war, almost one million people from all over Somalia have been forced to flee to Kenya, Djibouti, Yemen and Ethiopia. Those that went to Kenya travelled either by boat, car, or they walked. Some refugees from Mogadishu walked for up to 90 days in incredible heat to reach the Kenyan border. Many survived only by eating leaves from trees. Sadly, many died on the way.

It is hard to say who was worst affected by the refugee crisis. Most Somalis left their homes in a hurry, with no time to collect possessions or say goodbye to friends. Many families were split up and still live in the hope that they will one day be reunited. For the elderly it was particularly difficult. As one tired, starved and depressed old lady explained: "It is hard that I have lost my family, my home and my land. Now I arrive in Kenya. I have no clothes, I have to ask for my food, my shelter. I have lost my dignity."

By April 1994, the UN troops in Somalia had brought stability to some areas, although there was still fighting in Mogadishu and Kismayo. Some Somali refugees felt confident enough to return home, and two refugee camps in Kenya have since closed. One man, Mohammed Abdi, who has returned to the Gedo region of Somalia, expressed his feelings about going home like this: "Do I want to be in my home village? Of course I do. Living in a refugee camp is like living in a prison; you are given your food and shelter, but nothing else. You go mad just sitting. You spend your whole time dreaming of going home."

God is the greatest

Both paintings by Aden Ahmed Mohid, aged 14, Somali, Dagahaley refugee camp.

"We Somali children are Muslims. We go to Koranic school to learn about Islam. Here we stand in a circle singing inside our school."

Walking to Kenya

Shukri Jania Ebrahim and her travels

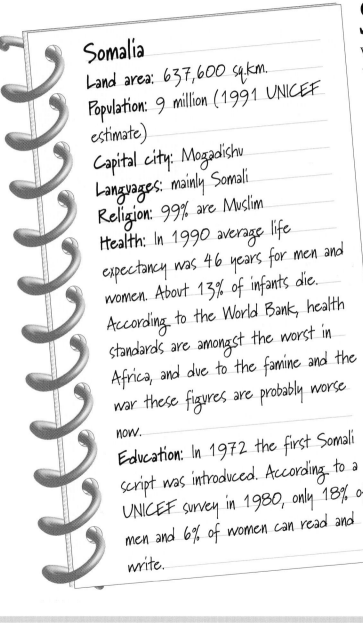

Somalia

Land area: 637,600 sq.km.

Population: 9 million (1991 UNICEF estimate)

Capital city: Mogadishu

Languages: mainly Somali

Religion: 99% are Muslim

Health: In 1990 average life expectancy was 46 years for men and women. About 13% of infants die. According to the World Bank, health standards are amongst the worst in Africa, and due to the famine and the war these figures are probably worse now.

Education: In 1972 the first Somali script was introduced. According to a UNICEF survey in 1980, only 18% of men and 6% of women can read and write.

Shukri comes from Somalia. When I first met her, she was with a large group of Somali women. She looked much older than 15. She was helping her mother to cook.

Shukri's mother is very reliant on her. While they lived in Nairobi, Shukri went to school. But now she stays at home to look after her mother.

The Somali women stick together for protection. They feel very vulnerable without the support of men.

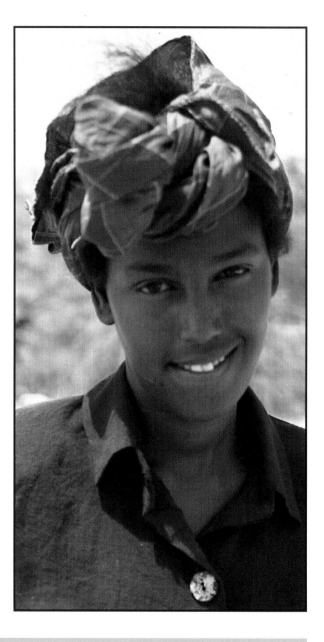

Shukri Jania Ebrahim, aged 15,
Somali, Haweia clan.

Shukri's journey

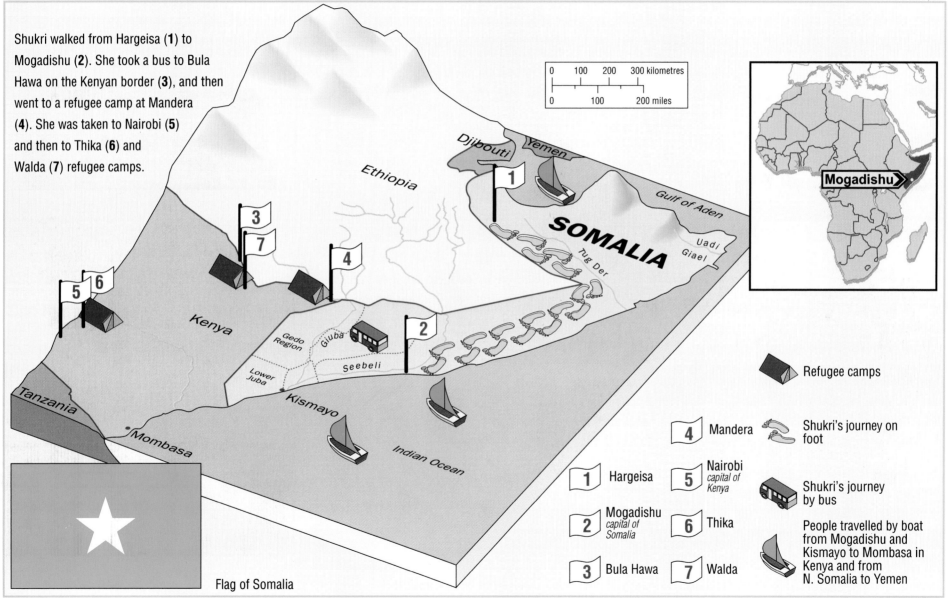

Shukri walked from Hargeisa (**1**) to Mogadishu (**2**). She took a bus to Bula Hawa on the Kenyan border (**3**), and then went to a refugee camp at Mandera (**4**). She was taken to Nairobi (**5**) and then to Thika (**6**) and Walda (**7**) refugee camps.

Ethiopia

Djibouti

Yemen

1

SOMALIA

Gulf of Aden

Uadi Giael

Tug Der

3

7

4

Kenya

Gedo Region

Giuba

2

Seebeli

Lower Juba

5 **6**

Tanzania

Mombasa

Kismayo

Indian Ocean

0 100 200 300 kilometres

0 100 200 miles

Mogadishu

Refugee camps

4 Mandera — Shukri's journey on foot

1 Hargeisa

5 Nairobi *capital of Kenya* — Shukri's journey by bus

2 Mogadishu *capital of Somalia*

6 Thika

3 Bula Hawa

7 Walda — People travelled by boat from Mogadishu and Kismayo to Mombasa in Kenya and from N. Somalia to Yemen

Flag of Somalia

I am the first-born

"We were among the first Somali refugees to come to Kenya. We used to live in Hargeisa which is in northern Somalia. My father was a very rich man; we lived in a villa. My father's clan is the Haweia. I think you know General Aideed who comes from my clan?

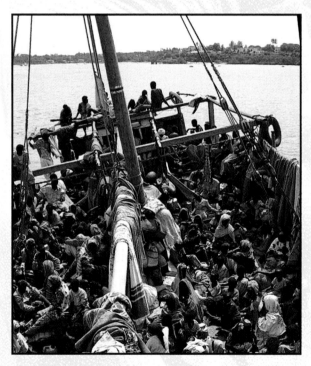

After 15 days at sea, a sailing boat arrives in Mombasa harbour. Crammed aboard are 378 hungry, thirsty and frightened refugees from Somalia.

One day, some men came to my house. They were not soldiers, they were dressed like you and me. They asked the last-born child who was only four years old, 'Is father in?' When my father heard it was them, he took me into another room and told me, 'These men have come looking for Somali National Movement people. They think I am one of them. This will be the last time I see you. Now you are the mother and the father.'

He gave me some papers which he said I should give to my mother so that she could get money from the people in town. Then my father met those men. My father told them, 'I will come with you. I don't want any fighting in front of my children.'

I asked the men, 'Are you taking him for good?' They told me, 'No, no, we are just going for a meeting.' I was the last person in my family to see my father.

> They told me, 'No, no, we are just going for a meeting.' I was the last person in my family to see my father.

The fighting was horrible. The government was looking for people belonging to the rebel group, the Somali National Movement; they were killing people, raping girls. Nobody cared because everybody was trying to save their own lives. We could not trust anybody as they were all scared of us because of father. Three days after they took father, Mama decided that we should leave Hargeisa and go to Kenya. I am the first-born, so I am responsible. We are nine children, three from my aunt who died. My Mama cannot live without me.

The first day of walking was normal for us, except for the sun made our legs feel swollen and awful. By the second day we were walking only at night because during the day the enemy was fighting and there were roadblocks on the road. It was the first time we had ever walked at night. We heard lions roaring, and we saw many snakes and scorpions. We didn't have any problems with the animals though, it was the people we were scared of. Some boys from Hargeisa walked with us. They had money and helped us to carry the little children. After three days, they bought two donkeys and the little children sat on the donkeys. Myself, I had to walk because I am the first-born. I used to put my feet in water when we reached a village at the end of the day. I would just fall down.

On the fourth day, my Mama became seriously ill. She was pregnant. Before, at home, she had to have an operation when she gave birth. She was in a lot of pain and we didn't know what to do. Luckily, a family in a Land Rover helped us. They took Mama in the car to Mogadishu and said that we must follow on our own. It took two days for us to walk to Mogadishu. They were very long days for me. If Mama died, then I had to look after all the children, and I didn't know where Kenya was.

I didn't know where Kenya was.

When we arrived in Mogadishu, the boys took us to the hospital where Mama was. She told us that her baby had died. She was very tired and had to spend one week in hospital. We stayed with relatives of the boys. I stayed with the three youngest at one place, and the other children stayed at another place. After one week, Mama came out of hospital. The doctors told her she must not walk or carry heavy things. But we had no home in Mogadishu, so what could she do? People gave us money, saying that we should go back home. We said, 'Yes, yes, yes,' and took the money to get a bus to Kenya. How could we go home?

People were very kind to us. When we were walking to Mogadishu, people in the ▶ p39

▲ The Somalian refugees build their own homes, which are called tukuls.
◀ A refugee camp in north-eastern Kenya. About 45,000 Somalis live here.

Travelling to the refugee camp

Painting by Binti
Aden Denle, aged
12, Ethiopian, Ifo
refugee camp.

villages gave us milk and meat. In Mogadishu, when we asked for help, people gave us money.

We took a bus to Bula Hawa, on the border with Kenya. By this time my bones were aching. I thought I was going to die. We were taken in a truck to Mandera refugee camp and I went with my mother to hospital. I had malaria, and my mother had stomach pains from her baby. The people in Mandera said it was very serious and we were transferred to Nairobi. We cried until all my brothers and sisters came too.

> By this time my bones were aching. I thought I was going to die.

We stayed in Nairobi for three years at Thika refugee camp. I went to school where I learned English. In 1992, we were transferred to Walda refugee camp. By this time, there were many Somali

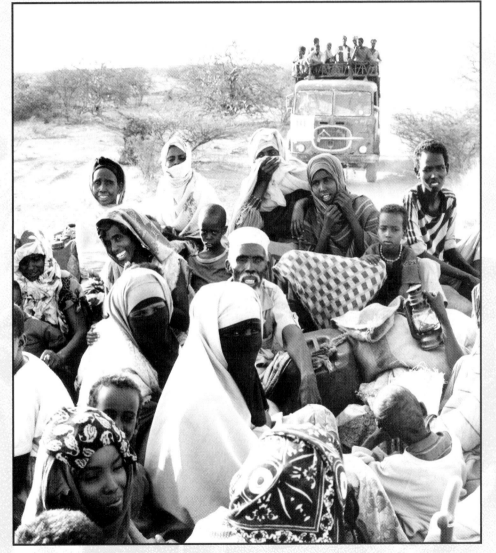

Somali refugees travelling by truck

refugees in Kenya because the country was totally messed up. We didn't like Walda, it was like a desert, but the people said that we must go to Walda so that we could plan for the future, so that we could be resettled. You see, we cannot go back to Somalia. People hate us in Somalia, and we have no home, no family, no nothing.

Last month, we heard news of my father. They put him in a hole for two years with no

I am the first-born

light so that he became blind. He was with eight other men. When the fighting became very serious in 1992 they stopped feeding him properly. When he came out of the hole, the woman told me he had scars all over his body. He died last month.

I am the first-born and I feel very sad. Life here is very hard. The life in Somalia was very different. This place is a jungle place. Even the way we looked before and the way we look now is different. I have a problem with the boys here. I will not get married or have a boyfriend because my Mama needs me. I don't think my Mama would survive without me. I have to look after my family first. I will feel threatened as long as I am without a father or brother to protect me.

I would like to tell you that my story is not the same for all Somalis. There were many who came to Kenya in 1992 when the fighting was very bad. They were starving and very sick. We were lucky, people helped us. But these people did not have anyone to ask for help. "

> **I am the first-born and I feel very sad. Life here is very hard.**

Women fight hard for their survival, and for that of their children. Without husbands or fathers to protect them, they are vulnerable to attack.

A food drop

Painting by David Deng Aleu, aged 16, Sudanese, Kakuma refugee camp.

"Everybody is happy about the food drop. I am watching. A blind lady is being helped by a small boy. People are jumping to catch food."

The deaf man and the blind man

Once upon a time there were two men, one deaf and one blind, who lived in the same town. One day there was fighting and the people of the town decided to move to another place. The deaf man saw everyone leaving, but didn't understand why. The blind man heard everybody leaving, but couldn't follow. They were both left feeling very sad.

Some people told the blind man where to go, but he didn't know how to follow his people because he didn't have any eyes. The deaf man couldn't hear the instructions of how to follow his people.

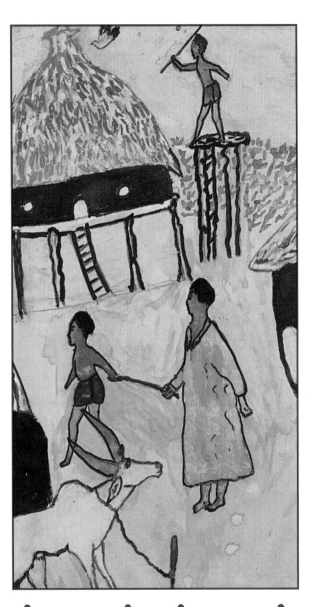

The blind man called for help, but the deaf man could not hear him. Luckily the deaf man saw the blind man. He took his hand, and using hand language they worked out where the people had gone. When they arrived in the town, the king saw them. He was amazed when he heard their story, and promised that they would never be left again.

Batula Mohammed Ali, aged 13, Somali.

Painting by Zekana Alien Deng, aged 15, Sudanese, Kakuma refugee camp.

Sailing from Kismayo

Both paintings by Said Abdi Said, aged 14, Somali, Dagahaley refugee camp.

"I lived in Kismayo until the fighting became very bad. Then I left with my mother, brothers and sisters. We had to pay to go on this boat with many, many other people. At night we were cold with the wind and during the day we were burnt by the sun. It should have been fun, but the old people were sick and we were leaving our home behind. For one day, OK - but two weeks...!"

"When we arrived in Mombasa we had to wait to be allowed into the country. It was terrible. I know that nobody wants refugees, but do they know that we don't want to be refugees?"

Ethiopia The past

Ethiopia has one of the richest and oldest histories in Africa. One legend says that the first Ethiopian ruler, Menelik, was a descendant of King Solomon of Israel and the Queen of Sheba. During ancient Greek times, Ethiopia was thought to be the place where the sun set. Throughout its history, high mountains have protected Ethiopia from attack by other countries. The first invasion that the Ethiopians experienced was by the Italians, in 1895. The Italian army was defeated but Italy kept some territory in the coastal area of Eritrea.

In 1935, the situation changed when Italy finally conquered Ethiopia. The emperor of Ethiopia, Haile Selassie, was forced to live in exile in Britain until, in 1941, British, Indian and Ethiopian troops drove out the Italians, and

Ethiopia became an independent country once again. However, the British ruled Eritrea until 1952, when an agreement was made to join the territory with Ethiopia. Under the terms of this agreement, Eritrea kept its own regional government.

Emperor Haile Selassie was killed in 1974 by a group of army officials who then took power. In 1977, Colonel Mengistu Haile Mariam became head of state and introduced a communist government which was supported by the (then) Soviet Union. During his 14 years in power, Mengistu built up a huge army and dealt ruthlessly with anyone who dared to question his government. Once, when a member of the government tried to question a policy at a meeting, Mengistu pulled out a gun and shot him on the spot. The whole country lived in

terror; over 100,000 people were killed, and thousands more escaped to neighbouring countries.

In the late 1970s, Ethiopia and Somalia started to fight over the Ogaden region. Hundreds of thousands of Somalis living in the region were forced to flee as refugees to Somalia. Backed by the Soviet Union, Ethiopia won the war.

During Mengistu's rule, and after, three rebel groups were active in campaigning against the government. Eritrea was made a province of Ethiopia in 1962, going against the agreement made for regional government in 1952. This led to the formation of the Eritrean People's Liberation Front (EPLF). A second opposition group, the Tigrayan People's Liberation Front (TPLF) fought for greater freedom in dealing with the affairs of the region of Tigray. The third group formed was the Oromo Liberation Front (OLF) in the south of Ethiopia.

Ethiopia suffered from serious droughts

Ethiopia The present

in 1973-4, 1983-5, 1987 and 1989-90. Civil war helped to turn these droughts into famines. Regions seen as 'rebel areas' by the government were deprived of aid. The famine in 1983-5 came to the world's attention following a news report on BBC television. Pop stars, led by Bob Geldof, took part in the 'Live Aid' concerts to raise money for aid for Ethiopia.

In May 1991, the Mengistu government was overthrown, and by July a new government was formed that included representatives from all the various movements in Ethiopia. At the same time, the EPLF formed a government in Eritrea and, in April 1993, Eritrea was pronounced an independent state. However, in Ethiopia disagreement about regional elections in June 1992 led to the OLF withdrawing from the state council. Fighting in southern Ethiopia followed, and many Oromo people fled to Kenya. An agreement between the Oromo and the government in November 1993 meant that these refugees could begin to return home.

Most of the 75,000 Ethiopian refugees living in Kenya returned home at the end of 1993. However, there are still about 5000 Ethiopian refugees in Kenya, many living in Kakuma camp. Most of them are 'political' refugees who claim that their lives would be threatened if they returned to Ethiopia. Many are interested in resettling in Europe or the USA. But every year, fewer refugees are accepted by Western countries. This means that most of the Ethiopian refugees living in Kenya will stay there until they feel safe to return to Ethiopia.

Until that time, the Ethiopian refugees in Kakuma have established their own community. It is interesting to see the way that, with exactly the same equipment, the Ethiopians build their homes in a totally different way from the Sudanese. Many Ethiopian homes have 'front rooms' built to provide a space for a shop. The Ethiopian quarter of Kakuma is the commercial centre of the camp. Here, there are shops, shoemakers and a 'Hotel Intercontinental'

Eritreans celebrating their independence in April 1993

where the Ethiopian refugees provide the entertainment.

Many of the Ethiopian refugees are professional, educated people. In Kakuma, they feel very frustrated. As one woman explained: "I fled from Ethiopia as a student. Now I am in Kakuma, in this heat, with no books and no work to do. I feel like I am wasting my life."

Nebiyou Assefa and his travels

Ethiopia

Land area: 1,223,000 sq.km.

Population: 52.7 million (1994 official estimate)

Capital city: Addis Ababa

Languages: Amharic, Orominya, Tigrinya, Afar, Somali and others

Religions: 40% are Christian, mostly Ethiopian Orthodox Church. About 45% are Muslim.

Health: Life expectancy for men is 46 years, for women 50 years (World Bank, 1990). There is one doctor for every 78,770 people, and one nurse for every 5390 people in Ethiopia (World Bank 1984).

Education: It is estimated that 38% of adults can read and write (World Bank 1985).

Nebiyou comes from Ethiopia. He is a shy boy with a good sense of humour. When I first met him he was painting in his hut. He was very bored because he had not yet been admitted to school.

Nebiyou lives with 42 other orphans. They have their own football team and music band. When I last visited him, I arranged for him to start carpentry lessons.

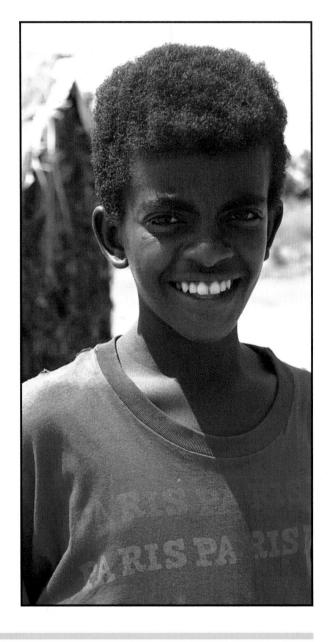

Nebiyou Assefa, aged 14, Ethiopian.

Nebiyou's journey

Nebiyou's route was from Addis Ababa (**1**) to Blate (**2**) with his father in a car. He went from Blate to Walda (**3**) in an army truck, and from Walda to Kakuma (**4**) in a UNHCR vehicle.

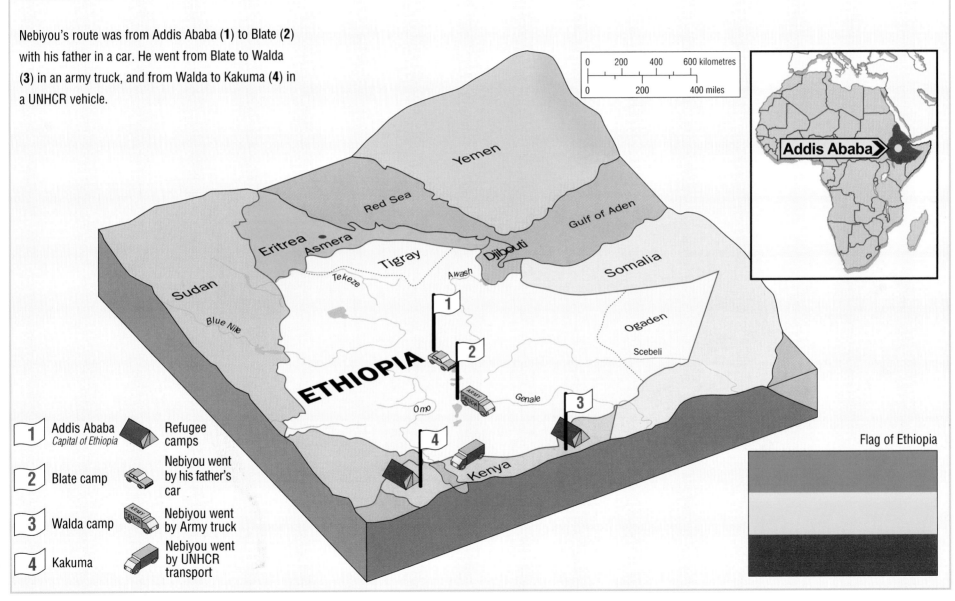

0   200   400   600 kilometres

0   200   400 miles

Addis Ababa

Yemen

Red Sea

Eritrea Asmera

Tigray

Djibouti

Gulf of Aden

Awash

Somalia

Sudan

Tekeze

ETHIOPIA

Ogaden

Blue Nile

Scebeli

Omo

Genale

Kenya

1 Addis Ababa
Capital of Ethiopia

Refugee camps

2 Blate camp

Nebiyou went by his father's car

3 Walda camp

Nebiyou went by Army truck

4 Kakuma

Nebiyou went by UNHCR transport

Flag of Ethiopia

Who cares anyway?

"My name is Nebiyou Assefa; Nebiyou for me, Assefa for my father. I am 13, no, 14 – well, who cares anyway? When I lived in Ethiopia I lived with my father who was a soldier in a military camp. Well, of course, I didn't always live there; I lived in Addis Ababa with my mother until she died when I was small. In Addis I lived in a house with toys and such happy things. When my mother died, my father came and said, 'Now you will live with me.' So we went to Blate military camp. You know it? I think it is very famous.

It is difficult for me to tell you about my life in Ethiopia because it was a long time ago. My father said to me, 'You eat, you go to school, and you sleep,' and I was happy just to play

Ethiopian refugees travelling by bus in Kenya

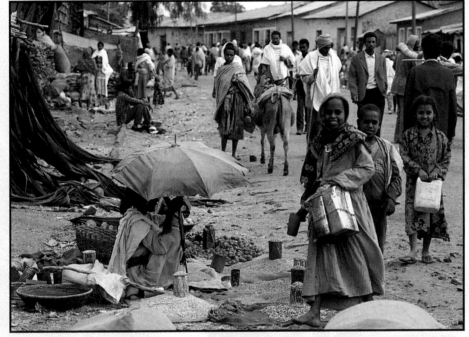

A market scene in Ethiopia

ence if my father is dead or alive. But, you see, at the same time President Mengistu was sent from the country. Everybody listened to the radio all the time, and the whole community, it changed. I walked around everywhere looking into doors. Nobody cared. Everything was messy, cars were driving everywhere. People were afraid of one another, and nobody wanted to look after me.

and be with my father. Then, I don't know, one day he went to the fighting place. From that time he didn't come back. A soldier told me, 'If he live, I don't know: if he die, I don't know.' Think of the soldier telling me this news just like that! I said that this is big news and there is a big differ-

I had no mother, no father, no friend even.

The soldiers said that this was very bad, that they had to go to Kenya to the refugee camps. I said, 'If they have to go, I have to go too.' You see, I had no mother, no father, no friend even. So it was by

chance that I came to Kenya. Of course, I didn't know how to get to Kenya, I didn't even know which direction it was in. ▶p54

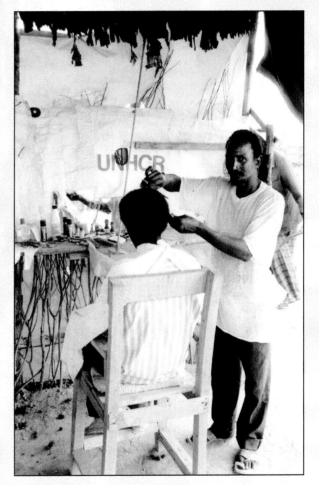

Having a haircut in the refugee camp

Ask the big people why

Painting by Liban Ahmed Habib, aged 10, Ethiopian, Ifo refugee camp.

"Don't ask me why I am a refugee, I don't know. Before we came here we lived with our camels. Now we live in a refugee camp. Soon we go home again. That is all - ask the big people why."

Children's faces in tents

Painting by Binti Aden Denle, aged 12, Ethiopian, Ifo refugee camp.

"All night we wait in tents for the day to come. This place is very dangerous, bandits attack us at night. I am showing the frightened faces of the children in our camp."

Who cares anyway?

I just heard people with families and soldiers talking about going to Kenya, and I knew that I must go too.

I came to Kenya in a big car. I wore a uniform and guns like the soldiers, and lay on the floor all the time. I wanted to live with them in the refugee camp in Kenya, but I am just a little boy and they said I had to live in the orphanage camp with the other orphan children.

We stayed in a refugee camp called Walda. Very soon, people did not like it because it was like living in a desert. So, so hot. You cannot think, you cannot eat, you cannot move. Other children were

Binti painting (see paintings pages 38 and 53)

lucky – they had a family, so when it was safe to go home they left with their families. They were happy to leave the desert. But us orphans? What about us? All that we could do was watch people go home and ask when we were going too. Our problem is that we love our country and want to return home. But we don't have parents, and because of that we can't go home.

Our refugee camp was closed and we were moved to a new camp called

> **Our problem is that we don't have parents and because of that we can't go home.**

Kakuma. It was very bad when we arrived in the new camp. It was raining all the time and we did not have time to build a new home. People came and took our photographs to send to the government in Ethiopia. They said we could go home if someone from our family saw the photograph in Ethiopia. But we are orphans, we have no family, so what are we going to do? I feel simply left here.

We do not want to go to a place without friends. I have a friend called Beruke Meles who is also an orphan. I will go any place with him. I cook for Beruke and he cooks for me. We only want to learn now. Firstly, I want to learn and secondly, if I can do it, I want to do the doctor's work. If I cannot learn that way, I will do something so that I can live in my own country. **"**

The wise and the foolish

In traditional Ethiopian society, bible students (Yekolo Temari) were known for their wisdom, as well as for their tricks and mischievousness. The bible students were always young men. They often lived with poor priests, so they had to find cunning ways to get food and money. Although the students were often troublesome, they were considered to be symbols of the future and of new ideas. They were responsible for not allowing Ethiopia to get stuck in its traditional old ways.

Once upon a time, there were two friends. One was a fool, and one was wise. They were both very poor. One day, the wise one decided to leave his home in search of fortune.

"I am tired of having no clothes and no food," he told his foolish friend.

After a few hours of walking, the wise one became hungry. His rumbling stomach made him start thinking about how he was going to find food. He went to the riverside, caught a frog and put it in his pocket. He soon reached a town. He went straight to the best restaurant in town and ordered the biggest meal on the menu. At the end of the meal, he ordered a bowl of soup. When it arrived and the waiter was not looking, he put the frog into the soup. Then he shouted,

"Waiter, waiter, there's a frog in my soup!"

The owner of the restaurant heard him shouting and begged him to be quiet.

"You will ruin me!" he whispered to the wise one. "I will pay you if you don't tell anyone."

So the wise one left the restaurant with a full stomach and full pockets.

When the wise one arrived home, the foolish one saw that his wise friend was wearing new clothes. As soon as the foolish one heard how his friend had made his fortune, he decided that he was going to do the same. He walked to the same town, finding a frog on the way. When he reached the town he went to the same restaurant and ordered the same meal. At the end of the meal he asked for a bowl of soup.

"Soup is finished," said the waiter.

"This is terrible!" the foolish one shouted. "Where am I going to put my frog?"

The owner of the restaurant heard him, and was very angry. The foolish one was beaten and sent from the town.

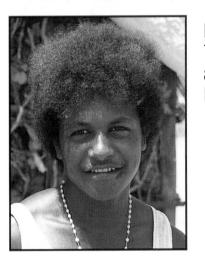

by Girma Tescaye, aged 14, Ethiopian.

Postscript: Rwanda 1994

On 6 April, the plane carrying the presidents of Rwanda and Burundi was shot down. From this point on, the world looked on in horror as more than 500,000 people, who were mainly from the minority Tutsi tribe, were murdered by people from the majority Hutu tribe.

On 28 April 1994, more than 200,000 Rwandans fled to Tanzania in what the UNHCR described as the 'largest and fastest' refugee exodus ever. The majority were from the Hutu tribe, who fled the advance of the Rwandan Patriotic Front (RPF), made up of people from the Tutsi tribe and moderate Hutus. Suddenly, Tanzania's second largest city was a refugee camp. Relief workers warned that if clean water and latrines were not provided speedily, a nightmare scenario of thousands of people dying of cholera and dysentery would be seen. Thankfully this did not happen in Tanzania.

On 14 July 1994 a nightmare of catastrophic proportions began when 1.5 million Rwandans began crossing into Zaïre following the victory of the RPF, and the setting up of a new government. One million people crossed into a tiny town called Goma. Within days the lack of clean water and sanitation led to a cholera epidemic in which people died by the thousand. Relief workers looked on helplessly as the unprecedented need for food, water, medication and shelter were impossible to meet in this isolated area. The international community responded by sending in large numbers of flights with relief assistance, but for the people with cholera, this was too late.

At the time of going to press, the Rwandan refugees in Zaïre remained in a pitiful state, dying by the thousand.

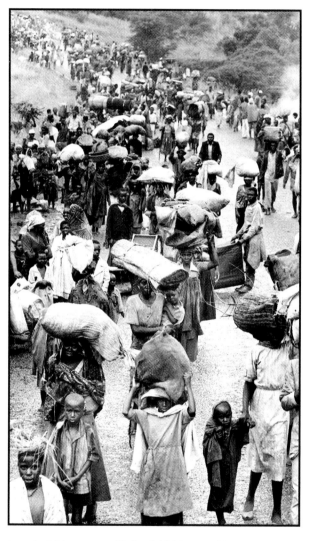

In only 24 hours, on 28 April 1994, over 200,000 people fled from Rwanda into Tanzania.

The United Nations High Commissioner for Refugees — UNHCR

'There is no greater sorrow on earth than the loss of one's native land.'
Euripides, 431BC.

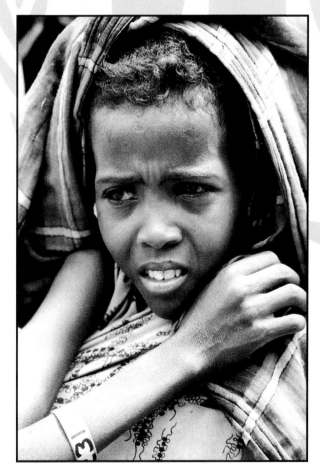

Young children often flee from their homes without knowing why they are going or where they are going.

In 1970 there were 2.5 million refugees in the world. In 1984 there were 11 million. In 1994 the number is 20 million, more than half being children. Helping the world's 20 million refugees is the job of the United Nations High Commissioner for Refugees (UNHCR) which was founded in 1951.

Wars, persecution and intolerance have always produced refugees. But the increasing number of refugees is a reflection of the instability of the world in which we live. The stories of Chol, Shukri and Nebiyou in this book echo the fate of numerous other children in wars raging around the world today. Children are often the main victims of war. They are killed and maimed during indiscriminate attacks on civilian communities. They also suffer from famine, malnutrition, disease and the trauma of being separated from their families. Those who survive are likely to be scarred for life.

Forced to flee from their homes out of fear for their lives, refugees often give up everything: home, belongings, family and coun-

try. They face an uncertain future in a strange land among people who do not always understand them. As a first priority, UNHCR gives protection to people from physical harm and from being forced to return to their own land. Relief assistance such as food, water, shelter and medical care is also provided. The children, the

Food distribution

The United Nations High Commissioner for Refugees — UNHCR

single women, the elderly and the disabled require special care.

Refugees are people just like you and me who, through no fault of their own, have been caught up in major upheavals. They are doctors and lawyers, farmers and fishermen, mothers, fathers and children. Albert Einstein and Sigmund Freud were refugees. What if the world had turned its back on them? Most refugees dream of returning with dignity and safety to live in their own country. When the longed-for day arrives, the UNHCR helps refugees to go home and to stop being refugees. But when the situation in their home country makes it impossible to return, people can remain as refugees for a long time. Only a very small number of refugees gets accepted every year to move permanently to a new country.

In a world where persecution, massive human rights violations and armed conflict remain a daily reality, the need to protect refugees is greater than ever before. Asylum for those who flee must be preserved.

Refugee houses

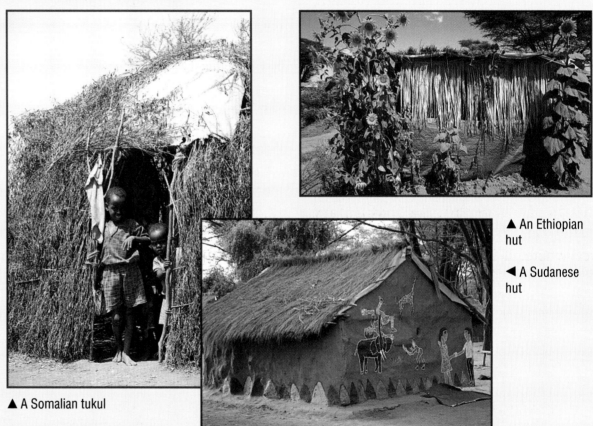

▲ An Ethiopian hut

◄ A Sudanese hut

▲ A Somalian tukul

The United Nations High Commissioner for Refugees supplies all refugees in Kenya with the same materials for building their homes. However, the final buildings look very different from one another, as the pictures above illustrate.

Save the Children Fund (SCF)

War, famine and the aftermath of conflict bring a terrible legacy of suffering for children. Thousands of children can find themselves suddenly refugees, cut off from their families and left to fend for themselves in alien environments where they are prey to death or disease, and often witnesses of torture and violence.

The Save the Children Fund in the UK is a member of the International Save the Children Alliance (ISCA). This is a worldwide association of voluntary organisations which works for children everywhere. It is committed to developing ways of bridging the gap between the delivery of emergency assistance to stricken communities and the impact of longer-term development projects. The problems must be tackled at every level. The improved coordination of different aid projects, more effective early warning systems, better needs assessment procedures, and the training of local people are all essential.

Working for the Swedish Save the Children Fund (also a member of ISCA), Rädda Barnen runs a number of programmes for the unaccompanied children in Kakuma refugee camp, northwest Kenya. One of the priorities of these programmes is to try to give back to the children their lost sense of security, discipline and responsibility. Adult refugees in the camp are recruited as supervisors for groups of up to 40 children. Their task is to encourage the children to be self-sufficient. In groups of six they build their own homes, cook their food and keep their living area clean and tidy. The role of supervisor is an important one: apart from monitoring the health and behaviour of the children, this network of trusted adults provides each child with someone to look up to, and to whom they can turn with any problems.

The Swedish Save the Children is also continuing the painting project set up by Sybella Wilkes and Sironka Averdung. Many refugee children suffer from forms of anxiety which they are more easily able to express through painting than in words. The project is a good example of the efforts being made by the Save the Children Fund to give children the opportunity to work through their problems and experiences in order that the rest of the world may try to understand and help.

Penny Tweedie / Save the Children Fund

Save the Children ⅄

Using this book in school

The 1980s and '90s have seen hundreds of thousands of people flee from their homes in the Horn of Africa, and the movement of refugees is likely to be one of the great moral and political challenges of the next century – a challenge for which young people must be prepared.

One day we had to run!, by use of its testimonies and cultural material, shows the effects of wars, environmental degradation and the abuse of human rights on the lives of ordinary children. Teachers can use the material in this book to enable students to explore concepts such as migration, justice, human rights, safety and the experience of being a newcomer. In particular, it can be used to teach the skills and concepts demanded by the National Curriculum as suggested below.

Whole school learning
The experiences of having to move recounted by the children in this book could be presented at school assemblies where the theme is homelessness, migration or refugees. The first-hand testi-monies and illustrations could also add an African dimension to group sessions with the aim of broadening the everyday experiences of young people. In this way, the book is a useful tool for strengthening the human rights ethos of schools.

Curriculum focused learning
The broad areas outlined here are directly applicable to the requirements of national curricula in the United Kingdom – as far as they were known at the time of publication.

For **geography**, this book provides authentic material to support lessons structured around themes of population movement, environmental protection and economic development. Close study of how and why children and families had to leave their homes in southern Sudan to flee to northern Kenya can involve mapwork skills as well as picture and discussion work on transport, homes and domestic economies.

For **history**, the colonial frontiers and the names of the countries in the Horn of Africa support work on wider world themes such as pre- and post-colonial African history, and larger movements of people over time.

For **religion**, the moral dilemmas related to war, violence and children's rights can be discussed through learning about the real experiences of children in difficult circumstances in one area of Africa. The situation in the Horn of Africa also provides scope for gaining an understanding of Christianity and Islam, and the interaction between these two major world faiths.

For **language**, the use of the children's own words adds to any exploration on the theme of childhood, or topic work on homes and journeys. Group discussion exercises could be devised to draw on the direct experiences and opinions of students in the class – for example, what personal objects we might take if forced to leave our homes in a hurry, or what memories we have of visiting or moving to a new country. The understanding that the testimonies in this book have been translated into English also provides scope for language awareness work on Arabic and the languages of Africa.

This book can also help to show the realities of problems faced by people in one part of the African continent in a way that avoids underlining negative notions of helplessness in the face of adversity. This is achieved through the quality of the first-hand testimony – presented at young people's own level of awareness – contained inside the pages of **One day we had to run!**

Schools with refugee children
More and more British schools are receiving refugee students from the Horn of Africa, particularly in London, Brighton, Cardiff, Liverpool and Manchester. Teachers using this book must be sensitive to the needs of these children when initiating classwork on refugees.

Refugee children may have experienced some of the horrific events described in this book. They may be unwilling to talk about their past as it might jeopardise the safety of family left at home, or because they do not want to feel embarrassed about the

Index

popular images of their countries.

However there are ways to make refugee children feel secure while at the same time increasing others' knowledge about their home country. One way may be to mount displays about life in a refugee child's country of origin. Parents and members of refugee community groups could also be invited into the school to tell folk stories and speak to students.

Further resources
Books for students

Eritrea: Africa's newest country Christian Aid. Although it is intended for use in primary schools, this book can also be used in geography lessons in secondary schools.

Refugees: a resource book for 8 - 13 year olds Refugee Council.

Voices from Eritrea and *Voices from Somalia* Minority Rights Group. A collection of testimonies of young refugees from these two countries.

Organisations

UNHCR (UK),
7 Westminster Palace Gardens,
Artillery Row,
London SW1P 1RL. 071-222 3065.

The Save the Children Fund,
Mary Datchelor House,
17 Grove Lane, London SE5 8RD.
071-703 5400.

Refugee Council,
3 Bondway, London SW8 1SJ.
071-582 6922.

Oxfam,
274 Banbury Road,
Oxford OX2 7DZ.

Christian Aid,
P.O. Box 100,
London SE1 7RT.
071-620 4444.

Catholic Fund for Overseas Development,
2 Romero Close,
Stockwell Road,
London SW9 9TY.
071-733 7900.

Minority Rights Group,
379 Brixton Road,
London SW9 7DE.
071-978 9498.

Haan Publishers,
197 Streatham High Road,
London SW16 6EG.
This organisation has produced many resources about Somalia including bilingual Somali/English resources for use in schools.